Hickory, Dickory Dock

and

The Cat Sat on the Rock

Notes for adults

TADPOLES NURSERY RHYMES are structured to provide support for newly independent readers. The books may also be used by adults for sharing with young children.

The language of nursery rhymes is often already familiar to an emergent reader, so the opportunity to see these rhymes in print gives a highly supportive early reading experience. The alternative rhymes extend this reading experience further, and encourage children to play with language and try out their own rhymes.

If you are reading this book with a child, here are a few suggestions:

1. Make reading fun! Choose a time to read when you and the child are relaxed and have time to share the story.

2. Recite the nursery rhyme together before you start reading. What might the alternative rhyme be about? Why might the child like it?

3. Encourage the child to reread the rhyme, and to retell it in their own words, using the illustrations to remind them what has happened.

4. Point out together the rhyming words when the whole rhymes are repeated on pages 12 and 22 (developing phonological awareness will help with decoding language) and encourage the child to make up their own alternative rhymes.

5. Give praise! Remember that small mistakes need not always be corrected.

First published in 2008 by
Franklin Watts
338 Euston Road
London NW1 3BH

Franklin Watts Australia
Level 17/207 Kent Street
Sydney NSW 2000

Text (The Cat Sat on the Rock)
© Brian Moses 2008
Illustration © Piers Harper 2008

The rights of Brian Moses to be identified as the author of The Cat Sat on the Rock and Piers Harper as the illustrator of this Work have been asserted in accordance with the Copyright, Designs and Patents Act, 1988.

ISBN 978 0 7496 8021 3 (hbk)
ISBN 978 0 7496 8028 2 (pbk)

Series Editor: Jackie Hamley
Series Advisor: Dr Hilary Minns
Series Designer: Peter Scoulding

Printed in China

Franklin Watts is a division of
Hachette Children's Books
an Hachette Livre UK company.
www.hachettelivre.co.uk

Hickory, Dickory, Dock

Retold by Brian Moses
Illustrated by Piers Harper

FRANKLIN WATTS
LONDON•SYDNEY

Piers Harper

"My favourite rhyme is 'The Owl and the Pussy-Cat' by Edward Lear because I like owls, cats, ships and the moon. I wish there was a nursery rhyme about chocolate."

Hickory, dickory, dock,

The mouse ran
up the clock.

The clock struck one.

9

8

The mouse ran down.

Hickory, dickory, dock.

Hickory, Dickory, Dock

Hickory, dickory, dock,

The mouse ran up the clock.

The clock struck one.

The mouse ran down.

Hickory, dickory, dock.

Can you point to the rhyming words?

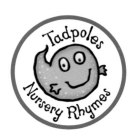

The Cat Sat on the Rock

by Brian Moses
Illustrated by Piers Harper

Brian Moses

"I don't have a cat but I do have a large golden labrador called Honey who barks loudly at cats whenever she meets them. Usually the cats ignore her."

Hickory, dickory, dock,

The cat sat
on the rock.

The rock was round.

The cat slid down.

Hickory, dickory, dock.

The Cat Sat on the Rock

Hickory, dickory, dock,

The cat sat on the rock.

The rock was round.

The cat slid down.

Hickory, dickory, dock.

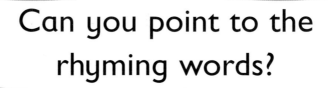

Can you point to the rhyming words?

Puzzle Time!

Can you tell the time
on these clocks?

Answers

Six o'clock

Half past four

Two o'clock

Twelve o'clock

Half past ten

Half past two